This book belongs to:

Interior Illustrations by Mary K. Biswas
Cover design by Tarique Khan
Book design by Opeyemi Ikuborije

Hardcover: 9781735738260
Paperback: 9781735738284
Imprint: LuntRidge Group LLC
DBA: Nonku's Corner Publishing
www.nonkuscorner.com

LIBRARY OF CONGRESS CATALOGING-IN-PUBLICATION DATA IS AVAILABLE

Printed in China

To Liam and Skylar

Each day you inspire me to celebrate myself and my story. Remember, celebrating your voice starts with knowing that you matter, and you have a purpose in this world. No matter where you go or what you experience, your voice will always be part of you. You have a purpose, and you are important. Always love and celebrate who you are.

To my husband

Your love and support made my lifelong journey a reality. I see and celebrate you just as you are. You are amazing.

To my family

Finding my voice has been a lifelong journey. You always believed in me and knowing that you were on my side helped me find my voice again. Tanatofu Mom.

To my dad, you inspire me every day to reach beyond the skies. Your wisdom and selflessness taught me so much about life and how to live without regrets. Your legacy lives on.

For the rest of my family, thank you for loving and supporting me unconditionally. You are my rock!

Nonku Kunene Adumetey

Perere
3/4/22

I Celebrate
My Voice

Illustrations by Mary K. Biswas

The world is full of many different voices. I celebrate mine.

What is my voice?

Is it what someone hears
when I speak?

Is it the signs I use to express myself?

Could it be what I want the world to see and know about me?

It is what I love to do, and it makes me happy.

I sing loud and free like a songbird.

The delight of singing is my voice!

Like a dinosaur,
I stomp hard and loud.

The courage to be bold is my voice!

I move and glide gracefully like a swan.

The fun of dancing is my voice!

Like a black marlin,
I swim lightning fast.

The thrill of swimming is my voice!

I am quick to run like a cheetah.

Reaching for the finish line is my voice!

Like a penguin,
I glide and slide happily on ice.

The joy of skating
is my voice!

Like an elephant,
I communicate in many ways.

Showing my feelings is my voice!

Like a golden eagle,
I reach for the sky.

I love and celebrate who I AM.

Like a butterfly spreading its wings,

I spread kindness wherever I go.

Like a tree, I grow and change
with every season.

So does my voice!

There are so many ways
to share our voices with
the world.

Some voices beat steadily like music,
making us twirl to happy rhythms.

Some voices create art and imagine stories.

Some voices help and heal,

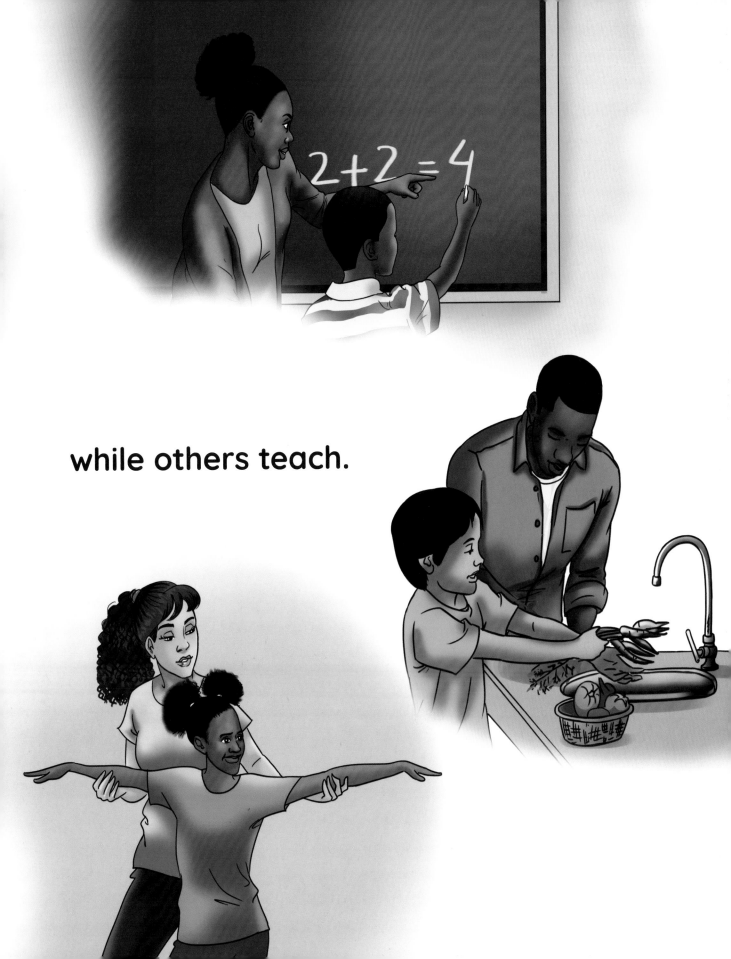

while others teach.

Our voices
show others
who we are,

what we believe in, and what makes us happy.

I am proud to share my voice
with the whole wide world.

It is beautiful,

limitless,

and all mine.

I celebrate my voice!

It is my superpower!

My voice is bold

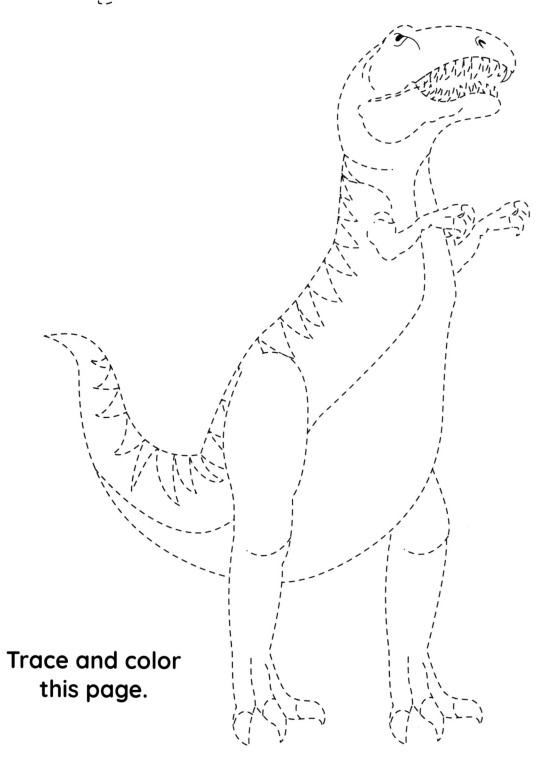

Trace and color
this page.

How do you celebrate your voice?

- -

- -

- -